Disney's
The Further Adventures of
Aladdin
3 A Small Problem

BY A. R. Plumb

ILLUSTRATED BY
Laureen Burger
Mark Marderosian
H. R. Russell

DISNEP
PRESS
NEW YORK

Look for all the books in this series:
#1 A Thief in the Night
#2 Birds of a Feather
#3 A Small Problem
#4 Iago's Promise

Library of Congress Catalog Card Number: 94-72228
ISBN: 0-7868-4023-4
FIRST EDITION
1   3   5   7   9   10   8   6   4   2

Disney's
The Further Adventures of

Aladdin

3 A Small Problem

"It's an awfully big desert," Princess Jasmine said to Aladdin. "I don't know how we'll ever find Mahdmani out here — especially in the dark."

Jasmine and Aladdin were riding on camels into the desert beyond Agrabah. Behind them rode Rasoul, the head of the Sultan's guard, and several of his men. Abu the monkey clung to the neck of Aladdin's camel. Iago the parrot fluttered overhead. The empty, dark desert surrounded them

all. The only light came from the yellow crescent moon in the black sky.

"Sand!" Iago said with disgust, looking around. "It's nothing but sand. I've never seen so much sand in one place."

"That's why they call it the desert, Iago," Aladdin said.

"Yeah, well, I'm with the princess on this one," Iago said. "There's no way we're going to find one evil sorcerer out here in the middle of nothing."

"There are rumors that Mahdmani's in

the area," Aladdin said. "We have to find him before he starts trouble."

Iago rested on Jasmine's shoulder. "Maybe he's gone home to wherever evil sorcerers go. Which is what I'd like to do. Go home. Take a bath. Wash this sand out of my feathers."

"You volunteered to come, Iago," Aladdin said.

"I *thought* it would be fun," Iago grumbled.

Jasmine frowned. "We don't even know what Mahdmani looks like," she said.

Just then Abu jumped onto the head of Aladdin's camel and pointed across the desert.

"Look!" Aladdin said. "It's a caravan."

In the distance a string of men and donkeys crossed the sand. Huge bundles were piled on top of the slow-moving animals. Behind the caravan Aladdin noticed a group of men on horseback. In their hands

were huge swords. The sharp blades glittered in the moonlight.

"Bandits!" Jasmine cried. "They're about to attack that caravan!"

Rasoul drew his own sword. "Those bandits will get quite a surprise when they discover that the Sultan's guards are here."

Aladdin nodded. "Let's go!"

Aladdin, Jasmine, and the guards raced their camels across the sand. The bandits were closing in on the caravan.

Suddenly their leader noticed Aladdin and the others. "Run for it, men!" he cried. "It's the Sultan's guards!"

The bandits turned and galloped off across the desert.

"After them!" Rasoul cried.

"No," Aladdin said. "Their horses are faster than our camels. We'll never catch them. Besides, we should see if anyone in the caravan is hurt."

Aladdin and Jasmine rode up to the caravan. A tall, thin man stepped forward. "I am Hammanid, the owner of this caravan," he said, bowing low. "You have rescued us from those foul bandits."

"Glad to be of service," Aladdin said.

"Traders must be able to travel in peace in my father's lands," Jasmine added.

"Your father?" Hammanid raised his eyebrows. "You are Princess Jasmine?" He bowed again. "Then I am doubly honored."

"Well, we'd better get going," Aladdin said. "We're looking for an evil sorcerer named Mahdmani. I don't suppose you've seen him?"

Hammanid shuddered. "An evil sorcerer? Certainly not. Bandits are bad enough for one night." He held up his hand. "But stay a moment. You must allow me to show my gratitude for your most courageous rescue."

Aladdin waved his hand. "No thanks are necessary. It was our pleasure."

"But I insist," Hammanid said with a frown.

Aladdin hesitated. The old caravan owner almost seemed angry. "Well," Aladdin said, "if you insist."

Aladdin and Jasmine climbed down from their camels. Hammanid led them to a donkey. On the donkey's back were two large barrels, one on either side. Hammanid told one of his men to unfasten the barrels. The men helped Rasoul and the other guards load the barrels onto one of the camels.

"Mine is a humble caravan," Hammanid said. "We do not carry gold or jewels."

"What do you carry?" Jasmine asked.

"Merely water, Princess. But . . ." Hammanid held up one long, thin finger. "It is the sweetest, purest, most perfect water in all the world. It comes from a far-off spring known only to me."

"Water?" Aladdin said, glancing at the barrels. Even though he hadn't wanted a reward, he had to admit he was a little disappointed.

"We gratefully accept this token of thanks," Jasmine said politely.

"Uh, yeah, that's right," Aladdin said. "Gratefully."

"You must share it with everyone at the palace," Hammanid said. "You will find even a small glass most refreshing. And a large glass . . . why, a large glass will make you feel young again."

Hammanid laughed loudly, as if he had just told a very funny joke. Aladdin and Jasmine watched the caravan depart. They could still hear Hammanid laughing as he disappeared into the black desert night.

Early the next morning, back at the palace,
the Genie tiptoed across a darkened room
to Aladdin's bed. He tapped Aladdin lightly
on the shoulder. "Wake up, sleepyhead," he
whispered.

But Aladdin didn't wake up. He just continued to snore. Loudly.

The Genie smiled. "Kid must have had a
tough night." He shook Aladdin a little
harder. "Rise and shine," he said softly.

Aladdin rolled over. He pulled the covers
over his head.

"Well," the Genie said with a shrug, "I tried it the gentle way."

Poof! He turned himself into an alarm clock so big it filled the entire room. The second hand swept around. With a deafening ***RRRRRIIIIIIINNNNNGGGG!*** that shook the walls, the alarm went off.

Suddenly the Genie became a huge blue rooster. "COCK-A-DOODLE-DOOO!"

Aladdin leaped out of bed. Abu shot out of his own tiny bed and into Aladdin's arms. They were halfway across the room

before Aladdin realized what was happening. He spun around and gave the Genie a dirty look.

The Genie became himself again. He smiled. "Too much?"

"Way too much," Aladdin said. "But I will admit one thing—it worked. I'm very, very awake."

"The Sultan wants to see you," the Genie said. "You're due in the palace dining room in . . ." The Genie checked a watch that had just appeared on his wrist. ". . . seventeen seconds."

"Seventeen seconds?" Aladdin cried. "I can't get ready in seventeen seconds! I still have to take a bath and brush my teeth and comb my hair and get dressed."

"No problem!" The Genie zapped himself into the black suit of a butler. "We'll have you ready in a jiff, sir," he said in a British accent.

Out of thin air, a blast of water drenched

Aladdin's pajamas. A toothbrush appeared in his mouth. It brushed away without any help from Aladdin. The Genie began blow-drying and combing Aladdin's hair. "Do you use a conditioner?" the Genie asked. "You can't be too careful in this desert sun."

Seconds later Aladdin was dressed and ready to go.

The Genie checked his watch again. "Four seconds to spare."

"How am I going to get to — ,"Aladdin began. But before he could finish his sentence, he, Abu, and the Genie were standing in the palace dining room.

"Never mind," Aladdin said. "I shouldn't have asked."

The Genie bowed grandly before the Sultan. "As you ordered, Your Highness. Here's Aladdin."

"Aladdin?" The Sultan looked puzzled. "Oh, yes, Aladdin, my boy. I did want to see you. But there was no need to rush."

"No need to rush?" Aladdin said, glancing at the Genie.

Abu scowled. He liked to sleep late.

The Genie grinned. "The early bird gets the worm, you know." In a flash of blue light, he turned into a bluebird and flew out of the room.

"I wanted to see you," the Sultan said to Aladdin, "because the cook has been asking about these barrels." He pointed to the barrels Hammanid had given Aladdin and Jasmine.

"Last night we saved a caravan from an attack by bandits," Aladdin explained. "The owner of the caravan wanted to reward us. He said this was the sweetest, most refreshing water anywhere. I guess it's from a special spring."

The Sultan opened the lid of the first barrel and peered inside. "It looks like plain old water to me."

"The owner seemed to think it was special," Aladdin said with a shrug. He wasn't interested in water. What he was interested in was breakfast. Now that he was awake, he was very hungry.

"Perhaps I should try some," the Sultan said. He picked up a ladle and dipped out some of the water. He took a sip. "Hmm, it

is very refreshing," he said. "In fact, it may be the most delicious water I've ever tasted. Would you like some?" He held the cup toward Aladdin.

"No thanks," Aladdin said. "But I'd love some breakfast."

"Cook!" the Sultan called out. "Cook! Some breakfast for Aladdin." He winked at Aladdin. "And I'll join you, my boy."

Safiya, the Sultan's head cook, came in from the kitchen. "But Mighty One," she said, "you've already had breakfast."

"Oh, yes, I'd quite forgotten," the Sultan said. He thought for a moment. "But it would be impolite not to join Aladdin. I'll just have to have a *second* breakfast."

Safiya nodded. "As you command, Sultan. And what shall I do with these barrels of water?"

"Why, serve us each a glass with our breakfast," the Sultan said. "That way everyone can enjoy it!"

While Aladdin was beginning his breakfast and the Sultan was beginning his *second* breakfast, Iago, Jasmine, and her pet tiger, Rajah, came into the dining room.

"Good morning, everyone," Jasmine said.

"Good morning, Jasmine," Aladdin said, smiling at her.

"Good morning, dearest," said the Sultan, taking a sip of water. "Did you sleep well?"

Iago flew to the table. "What? No good

mornings for me? What am I, part of the wallpaper?"

"Good morning, Iago," Aladdin said.

Iago plopped down in the middle of the table, fanning himself. "Whew, is it hot out there this morning. We're talking major scorcher." He grabbed the glass of water sitting in front of Jasmine and drank it down in one loud gulp. His face lit up. "Hey, that's not bad stuff. For plain old water, that is." He picked up Aladdin's glass of water and drank that, too. Then he dunked his beak into the water pitcher and slurped down some more.

Abu pointed to the empty glasses and shook his finger at Iago, chattering angrily.

"What?" Iago demanded, wiping his beak. "So I was thirsty. Since when is that a federal crime?"

"It's okay, Abu," Jasmine said. "I wasn't thirsty anyway."

"Me, neither," Aladdin said. He glanced

down at his empty plate and grinned. "I sure was hungry, though."

But Abu still looked annoyed. He grabbed the pitcher away from the parrot and took a long drink himself. He smacked his lips and smiled. Then he set down the pitcher, picked up a spoonful of porridge, and flipped it at Iago. Iago dodged in the nick of time, and the porridge landed on the floor. Rajah lapped it up eagerly.

"Did you see that?" Iago cried, pointing at Abu. "The monkey threw food at me!"

Abu put on his most innocent expression.

"No food fights, please," the Sultan said. "I'm trying to enjoy my breakfast in peace." He took another drink from his water glass. "Delicious! This really is the most refreshing water imaginable. You all must sample this."

Aladdin and Jasmine didn't answer. They were watching Iago try to drop a soft, ripe mango on Abu's head. Abu caught the mango and threw it back. It splattered on Iago's beak.

"Okay, that does it," Iago said, wiping his beak. "That definitely does it. You asked for it, you furry fleabag." Iago grabbed an entire plate of food and threw it at Abu. Abu was too busy laughing to duck.

Splat! The plate landed right on Abu's face, splashing food all over him. Abu shrieked with anger. Rajah tried to lick the food off Abu's fur, which made the little monkey even more furious. He lunged for a plate of lentils, accidentally knocking over the water pitcher and spilling the rest of the water. Rajah licked that up, too.

"Abu! Iago! Stop it, both of you," Aladdin said.

"You're acting like . . . like *animals*!" Jasmine added.

But it was too late. Food was whizzing through the air — lentils, strawberries, porridge, mangoes.

Suddenly the sound of swords being drawn met their ears. Rasoul and several other guards came rushing into the room.

"We heard a terrible battle!" Rasoul cried. "We came to save you, O Mighty Sultan."

The Sultan waved his hand wearily. "The battle you heard was a food fight." He pointed at Abu, covered with porridge. Nearby sat Iago, wiping mango off his feathers.

"Shall I take them out and punish

them?" Rasoul asked hopefully. "I could chop off their heads with a single blow."

"That might not be such a bad idea," Aladdin said, looking at Abu. Abu gulped and rubbed his neck.

"Head chopping?" Iago said. "Head chopping is so severe. My friend Abu and I were fooling around. Playing. No harm done, really."

Abu hopped across the table. He and Iago hugged each other like old friends.

"See?" Iago said. "Pals, best buddies."

"Look what you two have done with your fighting," Jasmine scolded. "You've made Rasoul and his men come running all the way up here. They were supposed to be getting the horses ready. We're going back to the desert today to look for Mahdmani."

"He started it," Iago said, pushing Abu away. "I was just sitting here minding my own business when the little monster started pelting me with porridge."

"Never mind who started it," the Sultan said. He turned to Rasoul. "My thanks to you and your men for rushing in here to save us, Rasoul. Please take a glass of this most delicious and amazing water to refresh yourself!" He gestured to Safiya, who quickly poured out glasses of water for the guards. "And take a pitcher for the rest of your men."

"Thank you, Sultan," Rasoul said, still glaring at Abu and Iago. He accepted the glass from Safiya and drank deeply. Then he did something no one had ever seen him do before — he smiled. "This is like no water I've ever tasted before!" he exclaimed. "It is so . . . refreshing."

"A small reward for your quick and faithful rescue," the Sultan said. "Even if it *was* only a rescue from a food fight."

After breakfast Aladdin and Jasmine went to the royal stables. They climbed onto their horses. "Are Iago and Abu coming with us?" Jasmine asked.

"Abu said he was, but I don't see him," Aladdin said.

Just then Abu appeared and scampered over to them. He leaped toward Aladdin's horse. To Aladdin's amazement, Abu missed and tumbled to the ground.

"Hey, what's the matter, Abu?" Aladdin

laughed. "You getting too fat from all this soft living?"

Abu frowned. He tried to straighten his fez. But the hat kept falling down over his eyes.

Just then Iago flew by. He was zooming at twice his usual lazy speed. "Okay, let's get going," he said. "I'm up for some serious desert flying today. I could fly clear to Damascus!"

Jasmine's mouth dropped open. "Iago?" she asked. That sure didn't sound like Iago. Iago usually complained about everything.

Rasoul arrived with his men. They were leading their horses. "Are you guys ready?" Aladdin asked.

"The palace guard is *always* ready," Rasoul said. For some reason his voice didn't sound nearly as gruff as usual. He started to mount his horse, but he couldn't quite reach the stirrup. He tried to leap into the saddle. But he slipped off and landed on his rear.

"You're as bad as Abu," Aladdin said with a grin.

Rasoul scowled. Abu scowled, too.

Rasoul took a running jump. At last he made it up onto his stallion. Abu grabbed the edge of Aladdin's saddle and pulled himself up. His fez was halfway down over his eyes.

"Is that a new hat?" Aladdin asked Abu.

Abu shook his head.

Aladdin lifted Abu's fez and carefully re-settled it on the monkey's head. It was the same old fez, all right. But now it was far too big.

Aladdin looked over at Rasoul astride his big horse. Rasoul's legs didn't even reach the stirrups. The rest of the palace guards' horses also seemed too large for their riders.

"What's going on here?" Aladdin asked Jasmine.

Jasmine shook her head. "Did all the horses grow bigger overnight?"

"That must be it," Rasoul said in his new, high-pitched voice.

"Why are you talking that way, Rasoul?" Aladdin demanded. He stared at the guard. "And what happened to your beard?"

Rasoul gasped. He stroked his chin. "I don't know!" he said.

Iago zoomed down and perched on the head of Aladdin's horse. "What is keeping you all? Are we gonna stand around here all week or are we going after Mahdmani?"

"Iago, what's wrong with your feathers?" Jasmine asked.

"Wrong? Nothing's wrong," Iago said. "My feathers are perfect." He held out a wing. "Look at those feathers. You'll never see better-looking feathers than these. All neat and clean and downy."

Iago froze. He stared at his wing. "*Downy?* Little chicks have down. I don't have down, I have feathers! Or . . . I *did*. Hey, what's going on here?"

"Yes, what *is* going on here?" Rasoul demanded in his high-pitched voice.

Aladdin looked at Jasmine. "Abu's fez is suddenly too big . . ."

"Rasoul and his men can barely get on their horses . . . ," Jasmine added.

"And Iago has feathers like a little chick. . . ."

"Plus," Jasmine pointed out, "he's suddenly full of energy."

"I know this will sound nuts," Aladdin said. "But it's as if all of them, Rasoul and Iago and Abu, have suddenly grown — "

" — younger!" Jasmine cried.

Just then a new figure emerged into the courtyard.

"Ah, there you are, Aladdin," said the Sultan in a high, clear voice. "I want you to talk to Nassir the tailor first thing tomorrow about making me some new clothes. It's the most curious thing. My diet must be working at last. Suddenly nothing fits!"

"Father!" Jasmine cried.

"Sultan!" Aladdin gasped.

The Sultan's magnificent turban covered his entire face. His expensive clothing hung in loose folds. When he walked, his feet kept popping out of his jeweled slippers.

"Father, you look so . . . so thin!" Jasmine said. She jumped off her horse and ran to the Sultan. Close up, she realized something else. He looked younger — *much* younger.

"Mew!" came a little voice.

30

Jasmine let out a gasp. A tiny tiger cub trotted over to greet her.

"Rajah!" Jasmine cried. She picked up the little tiger. "I don't think we're going after Mahdmani today," she said to Aladdin. "I think we have a big problem to deal with right here."

Aladdin nodded. "Or maybe it's more like a *small* problem."

"This is no time for joking," Jasmine said. "Everyone around us is growing younger. We've got to figure out what's going on!"

They all headed back inside. By the time they reached the throne room, the Sultan looked like a teenager. Abu couldn't stop bouncing and chittering. He was so small he could almost sit in his own fez. And Rajah couldn't stop chasing his own tail — a habit he'd long since outgrown.

Iago was in the worst shape. He could no longer fly — or talk. He had turned into a little chick covered with fuzzy down. Every now and then he let out a tiny chirp.

Aladdin sent Rasoul and the guards back to their posts. But they were now so young they could barely lift their huge swords.

"Father, this is terrible!" Jasmine said as the Sultan clambered up onto his throne. "Look how young you are. How can you rule Agrabah if you look like a teenager?"

"You're right," the Sultan cried. "I hadn't thought about that! What are we going to do?"

"Let's call the Genie," Aladdin suggested. "Genie! Genie!"

The room filled with a bright blue flash, and the Genie appeared. "What's up?" he asked. Then he looked at the Sultan. "Whoa! There must be something wrong with my eyes!"

Poof! A pair of thick glasses appeared on the Genie's nose. They made his eyes look huge. He peered at the Sultan.

"Genie, it's not *you*," Aladdin said. "This is real. Everyone's getting younger except Jasmine and me."

Iago hopped over and cheeped angrily at the Genie.

"Do I know you?" the Genie asked, scratching his head.

"That's Iago," Jasmine said.

"You look marvelous," the Genie told Iago. "I've never seen you look so young. No, really, I mean it."

"Genie, you have to help us stop this," Aladdin said.

The Genie zapped into a soldier in uniform and saluted sharply. "Yes sir! Right away, sir!" He closed his eyes, waved his arms around, and concentrated. "SHALA-MAZOLDA MAKUM OLDA!"

Nothing happened. The Genie opened one eye and peeked at his friends.

"Well?" Aladdin said expectantly. "They don't seem to be getting any older yet."

The Genie cleared his throat. "All right, let's take it once more from the top." He blew up to twice his usual size and waved his arms even more dramatically. In a deep, loud voice he boomed out, "HAKULA RAY-JUM GONNA AYJUM!"

Still nothing happened. "What's wrong, Genie?" Jasmine asked anxiously. "It's not working!"

The Genie grinned sheepishly. "Sorry, Princess. You know my powers aren't what they used to be before Aladdin set me free. I guess it's not going to work this time. The spell must be too powerful for me to break."

"You can't change me back?" the Sultan asked. "But how will I rule Agrabah?"

The Genie shook his head. "Sorry, chief. I wish I could help. I feel like a real heel." With a *poof*, he changed into a huge blue foot.

"Well, I'm glad to see your powers

haven't deserted you completely," Aladdin
commented, rolling his eyes.

"Who could have done this?" Jasmine
wondered, staring at her youthful father.

Zap! The Genie changed back into his
usual shape. "The old backward-aging rou-
tine?" He thought for a moment, then
snapped his fingers. "I've got it!"

"Who did it, Genie?" Aladdin asked.

"Someone not very nice," the Genie said.
"Yes, I'm sure of it. Someone not very nice
at all did this. You can count on it."

Jasmine sighed and looked around.
"Where's Iago?" she asked.

"He was over there a few minutes ago."
Aladdin pointed to an empty chair.

Then he realized the chair wasn't *completely* empty. There was something small and round and white sitting on the cushion.

Aladdin and Jasmine hurried over to take a closer look. The object on the cushion was a little egg.

"Iago!" Jasmine cried.

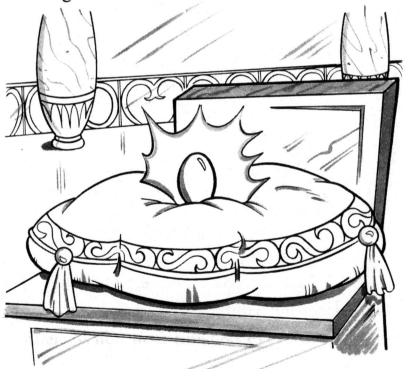

"Iago got so much younger that he became an egg again!" Jasmine exclaimed.

Zap! The Genie was wearing a chef's hat and holding a frying pan. "Omelette, anyone?" he asked.

"Wait a minute," Jasmine said. "Why did Iago get so much younger so fast? Abu hasn't changed much in the last hour."

Aladdin lifted up the tiny monkey and looked at him closely. "You're right. He's stopped getting younger."

"And Father seems to have stopped, too," Jasmine said. "So has Rajah."

Poof! The frying pan disappeared, and the Genie turned into a blue Sherlock Holmes. He pulled out a magnifying glass and stared at the Sultan. "Egad!" he cried. "I've discovered something."

"What?" Jasmine asked.

"Your father has a little piece of spinach stuck in his teeth," the Genie announced.

Aladdin rolled his eyes. "Genie, this is serious. We have to figure out how to undo this spell. We can't leave Iago as an egg."

Abu looked at the egg, then up at Aladdin. He nodded hopefully.

"No, Abu," Aladdin said. "It would *not* be a good idea."

Jasmine shook her head. "Aladdin, the real mystery is why you and I haven't changed. If we figure that out, maybe we'll understand what happened."

"You're right, Jasmine," Aladdin said.
"Of course, that's easier said than done."
He slumped to the floor. "I'm worn out
from all this. Plus, thanks to a certain large
blue someone, I didn't get enough sleep last
night."

The Genie turned himself green and
looked around innocently. "Large blue
someone?" he asked.

"You should have a glass of that excellent water we had at breakfast, my boy,"
the Sultan suggested. "It's most refreshing.
That will perk you up."

"Coming right up," the Genie said. He
disappeared. In a flash he was back with
two glasses of water. He gave one to Jasmine and the other to Aladdin.

Aladdin drank down half the glass at one
gulp. "Hey, this water *is* refreshing," Aladdin said. "I didn't have any at breakfast."

Jasmine took a long drink, too. "You're
right, Father," she said. "It's wonderful."

Suddenly Aladdin and Jasmine stared at each other.

"*You* didn't have any of the water at breakfast?" Jasmine asked Aladdin.

"And neither did *you*?" Aladdin asked Jasmine.

"That's it!" Jasmine cried. "The water is enchanted! That explains why Iago changed so much more than the others. Remember? He drank at least twice as much as anyone else."

"Ah, the old enchanted-water-from-the-fountain-of-youth trick," the Genie said, nodding. "Only a real sorcerer could have done this."

"But we got the water from Hammanid —the man who owned the caravan," Jasmine said. "He gave it to us as a reward after the caravan was attacked by bandits."

Aladdin frowned. "Was the caravan *really* being attacked by bandits? Or was it all a clever trick? Maybe Hammanid *arranged* to be attacked by men dressed up as bandits. That way he knew we would rush in to save the caravan and he could give us the water as a reward."

"But why would Hammanid do that?" Jasmine asked. She frowned. "Hammanid." She repeated the name slowly. "Wait a minute! What do you get if you rearrange the letters in *Hammanid*?"

Instantly the Genie made big alphabet blocks appear in the air. He twirled and rearranged them like a magician doing a card trick. "Mam Handi," the Genie cried. "That's it. Hammanid rearranged is Mam Handi!"

"Try again," Jasmine said.

The Genie reshuffled the blocks.

"Stop right there!" Jasmine said.

The letters froze in midair. "Mahdmani!"
Aladdin cried.

"So Hammanid is really Mahdmani the evil sorcerer," Jasmine said.

Just then Rasoul came running into the room. He looked about ten years old. His sword was dragging on the floor.

"O Mighty Sultan," Rasoul cried. "There is a man at the gate. He says he wants to speak to you."

"Send him away," the Sultan said. "We're busy here."

Rasoul shook his head. "He says he won't take no for an answer. There are many armed men with him. And the palace guards can't stop them. Most of my men are too young and small even to draw their swords."

"Who is this impertinent man?" Jasmine asked.

"He is the same man who led the caravan in the desert," Rasoul said.

"Mahdmani!" Aladdin cried.

"Mahdmani!" Aladdin pounded his fist against his palm. "This was his plan right from the start. He got us to drink the water, and now we're defenseless against him."

"Aladdin," Jasmine exclaimed. "My slippers are starting to feel a little loose."

Aladdin nodded. "It's started. See?" He gestured to his pants, which were much baggier than they had been a few minutes earlier. "We're beginning to grow younger. We need a plan, and we need it quick!"

"Genie!" Jasmine said. "You can get rid of Mahdmani."

The Genie nodded eagerly. "Let's see," he said. He snapped his fingers, and a large map of the world appeared in his hands. "I could transport him to Bora Bora, I suppose . . . maybe Shangri-la . . ."

"Hold on! Just getting rid of Mahdmani isn't what we need," Aladdin said. "We need to get him to undo this spell and return us all to our normal selves."

"But how?" Jasmine said.

Aladdin snapped his fingers. "I have an idea!" he said.

Just then the doors of the throne room flew open. A man swaggered in, laughing loudly.

"Mahdmani!" Jasmine said.

Instantly the Genie poofed himself into servant's clothes so the evil sorcerer wouldn't notice him.

"Yes, it is I, my dear little princess,"

Mahdmani said with a cackle. "I hope I find you well, young lady. Sultan! You amaze me. I thought you were a much older man." He laughed loudly at his own joke. "And of course I've already met the terrible Rasoul." Mahdmani patted Rasoul on the head. "What a cute kid."

"What exactly do you want here, Mahdmani?" the Sultan asked.

"What do I want?" Mahdmani laughed. "I want *everything,* of course. I want all of Agrabah. And who can stop me now?"

"I can try," Jasmine said angrily.

"Ignore her," Aladdin said. Quickly he

stepped in front of Jasmine. "She doesn't mean it. I mean, you're obviously in charge around here, Mahdmani."

"I'm glad to see you recognize the truth of your predicament," Mahdmani said.

"Hey, things change, right?" Aladdin grinned. "Out with the young"—he pointed at the Sultan—"and in with the new." He bowed low before Mahdmani.

Jasmine had no idea what Aladdin's plan could be, but she decided to play along. She just hoped he knew what he was doing. "On second thought," she said, "perhaps Aladdin has a point. We are helpless against your great power." She bowed, too. "I await your command, O Mighty One."

"Excellent," Mahdmani said, rubbing his hands together. "First, bring me the Sultan's jewels."

Aladdin turned to the Genie. "Bring the Sultan's jewels to Mahdmani. Immediately."

"While we're waiting for the jewels—,"

Mahdmani began. But before he could finish his sentence, the Genie was back. He was carrying several large chests.

"How did you get those jewels so quickly?" Mahdmani asked the Genie.

"I try to stay in shape," the Genie said modestly.

Mahdmani opened the chests. "All mine!" he cried. He dug his hands deep into the piles of sparkling rubies, emeralds, and diamonds.

"Hey, the whole palace is yours," Aladdin pointed out. "The royal throne room, the royal kitchen — "

"The kitchen?" the Sultan said, looking depressed.

"Come to think of it, I *am* famished," said Mahdmani. "You can really work up an appetite taking over a kingdom." He let out a cackle.

"Well then, you're just in time," Aladdin said. "The cook just whipped up a big batch of his specialty."

"His specialty?" Mahdmani repeated, looking interested. "What's that?"

"It's a special soup," Aladdin said. "A soup fit for a sultan. It's a secret recipe. Princes and noblemen travel for miles across the desert just for a spoonful."

"A spoonful, eh?" said Mahdmani with another cackle. He rubbed his stomach. "Well, I'll have more than a spoonful. I want the whole kettle!"

"I don't blame you," Aladdin said. "Our cook, Genie . . . uh, I mean, *Gene* . . . is a whiz in the kitchen." Aladdin turned to the Genie. "Why don't you show the new sultan to the dining room? Then," he added with a big wink, "serve him a big bowl of Gene's extra-special soup."

"Something wrong with your eye, kid?" the Genie asked loudly.

"No," Aladdin said. "I was just telling you to make sure the new sultan gets a *big*

bowl of that *special* soup." He winked
again.

"Oh! Well, you don't have to hit me over
the head," the Genie grumbled. "I can take
a hint." He bowed low to Mahdmani.
"Right this way, O Most Putrid One."

"Bring all of *my* new jewels along. And

I'll take that, too," Mahdmani said, pointing
at the ring on the Sultan's finger.

"But this is the Mystic Blue Diamond,"
the Sultan exclaimed. "It's been in my fam-
ily for years!"

"Yes, I know," Mahdmani said. He
snatched it from the Sultan's finger and slid
it onto his own. "Ah, a perfect fit."

A few minutes later the Genie, still dressed as a servant, set a silver platter on the dining table before Mahdmani. On it was a kettle of steaming soup, a bowl, and a large glass of water.

Mahdmani took one look at the glass and burst out laughing. "You must think I'm an idiot!" he cried.

"Well, now that you mention it . . . ," the Genie began.

"To imagine that I would fall into my own trap!" Mahdmani tossed the water into a nearby vase of flowers. Slowly they began to close until they were nothing more than tiny buds.

"You see?" he said to the Genie. "I'm not the fool you take me for."

The Genie shrugged. "Hey, you can't blame a guy for trying."

Mahdmani sniffed at the soup. "Mmm. This smells wonderful."

"Why, thank you," the Genie said, filling Mahdmani's bowl with soup from the kettle.

"Why are *you* taking credit?" Mahdmani asked suspiciously.

"Me? Oh, no reason." The Genie laughed. "I mean, it's not like I just zapped it up out of thin air or anything. Nope. I'm just a regular, everyday servant. No magic powers at all."

Greedily Mahdmani gulped down the soup. Then he had another bowlful, and another. When he'd finished every drop in the

kettle, he leaned back in his chair with a satisfied sigh. "Delicious," he said. "Being sultan is even better than I imagined. Finally, I have everything I ever wanted. Even the Mystic Blue Diamond."

Mahdmani held up his hand to admire the ring. Then he frowned. "It seems loose. Funny, a little while ago it fit perfectly. Now I could swear it's larger."

Aladdin, Jasmine, and the others joined the Genie in the dining room. "Afraid not, Mahdmani," Aladdin said with a grin.

"The ring hasn't gotten bigger," Jasmine said. "You've gotten smaller. Or should I say *younger*?"

"You've just consumed your own magic water," Aladdin added.

"Ah, but that's where you're wrong, boy!" Mahdmani said. He gestured to the flower buds. "I didn't fall for your pitiful trick."

"By the way," Jasmine said with a smile. "How did you like the soup?"

"Deli—" Mahdmani's eyes widened. "No! You put the magic water in that soup?"

The Genie zapped himself into a chef's

outfit and tapped Mahdmani on the shoulder. "The recipe's simple, really," he said. "You just take some eye of newt and tongue of bat, add a pinch of this and that. Bring to a boil, stirring often. Then add one quart of magic water from the evil loony. Voilà!"

"You won't get away with this!" Mahdmani shouted. But his voice had grown high and shrill as he continued to grow younger. "I know how to undo the spell."

"We were counting on that," Aladdin said. "You'd better hurry, Mahdmani. You had an awful lot of that soup. You wouldn't want to shrink away to nothing, would you?"

Mahdmani glared at Aladdin with hatred. But it was hard for him to look very scary when he was getting younger and smaller with every passing second.

"Well?" Jasmine said.

Mahdmani grumbled. He began to chant a spell. *"Alaka tubee miole seffa gen,"* he said slowly. Suddenly he was an old man again.

"Those are the magic words," Aladdin said.

"Try saying them, Father," Jasmine said.

"Alaka tubee miole seffa gen," the Sultan said. In a flash he was back to normal. He patted his round stomach. "It's me again," he said happily. "All of me!"

Aladdin picked up Abu. Jasmine picked up Rajah. Together Aladdin and Jasmine chanted the spell. In the blink of an eye they were all back to normal.

The Sultan marched over to Mahdmani. "I'll take the Mystic Blue Diamond back again, if you please."

Mahdmani hesitated. Just then Rasoul and his men arrived, summoned by the Genie. Jasmine told them the spell. One by one they repeated the magic words.

"Father's ring," Jasmine repeated to Mahdmani. Rasoul drew his sword. He had returned to his usual size, and he towered over the sorcerer.

"I'd be happy to return your ring, Sultan," Mahdmani said quickly. "It was all just a terrible mix-up." He handed the sparkling Diamond back to the Sultan. "A misunderstanding, I tell you."

Rasoul and his men led the protesting sorcerer away. The Genie turned back into his usual blue self.

"Good work, Genie," Aladdin said.

"Aw, shucks," the Genie said. "You cooked up the plan, kid. I just made the soup." He zapped up a gold medal with the word *Hero* engraved on it and hung it around Aladdin's neck.

Aladdin pulled a small white egg from his pocket. "I guess we'd better bring Iago back now." He said the magic words over the egg. In the blink of an eye Iago was back.

"It's about time!" he shouted. "I thought I was going to be stuck in that egg forever. Did you have to leave me till last? What, you didn't think I wanted to come out? You even fixed that stinking ape before me!"

Abu's eyes narrowed. He scampered out of the room and returned a moment later with a big glass of water.

"If I were just a little more sensitive, I might take offense," Iago continued. "Imagine, you fixed that fuzzy flea farm before me — that repulsive primate — that — "

Before Aladdin could stop him, Abu let the water fly. Most of it splashed right into

Iago's open mouth. Iago gulped and glared at the monkey. "That better not have been that magic water, fleabag," he said angrily.

Abu grinned and nodded.

"You rotten little rodent!" Iago sputtered. "I'll fix you good, banana breath. Just you wait."

"You know, you really shouldn't get so upset about these things, Iago," Aladdin said. "You'll only egg him on."

"Now, Aladdin," Jasmine scolded with a smile, "this is a serious matter. You shouldn't yolk about it."

Iago groaned and rolled his eyes. "This time do me a favor, okay?" he said as he began to shrink again. "Just leave me in there!"